Lulu Press

The Redemption of D.C. Hayes

A Darkness Rising Universe Novel

Written by: Alexis Allinson

Editors:

Jeffery Snow and Brian Niedzwiecki

Copyright 2012

ISBN # 978-1-300-10813-9

2nd Edition Print

Dedication

To my loving husband Mike:

One body, one soul and one brain! :P

Also to my children,

Aleena, Marcus, Akki and Ares:

Without all of you I would have no inspiration to write.

Prologue

Fenris, the large black wolf son of the Norse God Loki, walked up to his father within the middle of the woods in the place known as Midgard.

"You look worn out, my son," Loki proclaimed as he locked eyes with the wolf. Loki did not budge from his seat by the Potomac River.

Fenris snorted and huffed back. He wandered to sit next to Loki on the river bank. He was not in the mood for light conversation. It had been a long night already and he could sense it was only to become even longer.

Loki ignored the obvious attitude the wolf had wrapped himself in. "Has the deed been completed?"

Fenris nodded his large head and snuffed again in a throaty way.

"And the pup?" pressed Loki.

Fenris spoke in the language adopted by the Garu, known to the uneducated as werewolves. His soft reply was, "It is a male offspring. The pack has given him the title of 'Death Cub'."

Loki looked onto the face of his son with pride. "My grandson has been given a suitable name I take it?"

"He tore himself savagely from his mother's womb in the Fenril form of the Garu as a way of announcing his arrival into their pack."

Loki smiled. "What a wonderful and chaotic way to enter the world. The carnage must have been beautiful and magnificent to witness."

"His birth was provoked by Diana and the rising of her Super Moon, "Fenris commented. "She was provoked by the Olympian beast Eris. Eris was backed by her brother Ares. It was a sport between the siblings to see if they could cause a bit of anarchy and chaos within the heavens."

"Wonderful!" Loki danced in his seat as he heard Fenris' words. "A new demi-god has been unleashed onto Midgard and neither God nor Gaia was able to stop it. To have help from those residing in another rim of the Heavens; only makes this event even more smashing."

Loki rose from his spot and filled his lungs with night air and looked up at the moon. He raised his right hand and pressed it to his lips.

He then softly blew the kiss into the air towards the moon. "Thank you, marvelous Diana for the gift of your moon to mark the birth of my grandson. I am indebted to you for such a wonderful gift."

Fenris laid his head on his paws and ignored the rants of his father. The God was mad. He was also his father. For this, Fenris had the upmost respect.

Loki, annoyed at his son's lack of enthusiasm over the coming of his grandchild, turned back to him, not wanting to see his son's actual reaction for the fact that he did not care what it was. He asked, "How does his "*pack*" perceive this God among them?"

This made the wolf lift his head and body from the ground. Loki could sense the unease coming from his child. Fenris snarled with upset, "They think of him as a "*dog*" and have chased him away," he huffed. "It won't be long before they decide that his blood carries "*Bane*" and they send out their hunting party to track him down and kill him."

Loki quickly turned on the ball of his foot to face Fenris. "Oh," Loki sounded with obvious disappointment. "That won't do."

Fenris continued, "I chased him away from the remains of his mother and onto a farm and pushed him inside of a haystack. I think that will do until morning."

Loki clapped his hands, "Well...now that is a perfect place for him to grow!"

Fenris snuffed. It was obvious

that his father allowed his insanity to burrow into his head. "How can a haystack be a place for him to grow?"

Loki grinned, "Where there is a haystack there is a farm. Go to my grandson; your child and protect him from the pack for one year. Make the people on the farm take him in and keep him."

Fenris quizzically looked at his father. "A year is a long time for a God of the Garu to desert the pack."

Loki looked angry. "You will leave for one year. Let them call your brothers, Romulus and Remus. Let them call upon their fathers God and Seth. Let them beg to their mother Gaia. They have offended their brother Fenris by turning on their own God's offspring! They have offended me, Loki, their third father by not recognizing my grandson as a God placed among them for the battle that must be won. Allow them to be at the mercy of their half breeds they look down upon. "

Fenris turned to leave and then looked back upon his father. "What if Odin and God frown upon your decree?"

Loki smiled devilishly at the wolf. "What are they going to do? Tie me to a tree again for being a bad boy?"

With that, Fenris, the large, black ghost wolf, son of Loki and father to a half mortal son deemed a "Death Cub" was running off to where he left the cub in the hay as a full grown man in appearance.

Loki smiled with pleasure as he stepped onto the Rainbow Bridge and back to Asgard.

Chapter 1

D.C. held his head in his fur covered hands and howled. The images would not leave his sight. The rain pouring onto his body didn't remotely seep into his thoughts. With every flash of lightning he saw the horrific scene again.

The female wolf with the grey fur, ripped apart from rib cage to hip bone. Her flesh clawed from her. Her blood could be seen leaking out onto the ground. Everything illuminated from the full moon above. Her eyes held open in the horror of her own death. Looming in the shadows was the giant black wolf with the yellow eyes. The wolf was neither corporal nor wraith. He hissed and nipped and uttered the words that would haunt

D.C. for the rest of his life. The words D.C. heard on many hunts later and came to recognize as his branding.

D.C. closed his eyes tightly. The image was always stronger on a storm-filled night which didn't make any sense. He knows this image like the half demonic skin he is forced to wear. It happened, or will happen, on a clear night with a full moon above. His memories were always a jumble. He was truly cursed. The hardest part was that D.C. did not know if the deed was already committed or if it taunted him from the future. Sometimes he'd have dreams only for them to take place a day or two later with the same events. Mildred had told him he suffered from Déjà vu. Clive told him he ate something bad before settling down to sleep.

Sitting in the mud he finally

stopped his whimpers to look up. The heavy rain drops mixed with his tears and both washed away together.

"Death Cub," were the words the apparition had called him when he was first discovered hiding in the bush just beside the corpse of the slaughtered bitch. The name was suitable. The others who had arrived shortly before the apparition had also given him this designation. He didn't understand any of the rest of their yips and yowls. He did understand their growling and sudden chase they gave to rid him from their pack. They gave up the chase long before the ghost did. That had flung him out of the woods and into the haystack on the farm. The farm his spent the last year on.

The first howls pursued him in his brain. Then the calls filled his ears. That is when he noticed the hunting party that was out looking for him was closing in on his location. They yipped, yowled and growled as they came closer. D.C. used his instinct to run, but his legs didn't feel strong. He thought he saw the giant black wolf nipping at his heels to force him into moving faster. His mind was too shredded to be sure that it actually existed. He also didn't wish to slow down to find out.

D.C. had learned over the last year since being discovered in the hay at the old farmer's house that he wasn't like the "*people*" he was exposed to. The old man, Clive and his wife, Mildred, said it themselves when D.C. learned to communicate properly to them that he was like a "Werewolf from a movie or something." D.C. had become somewhat comfortable with this persona as it kept others who would come out to the farm or who he would see in town at a distance. He liked being alone. Unfortunately being alone also meant he had to deal with the memories of the slain she-wolf in the woods.

D.C. shook his head. The pack was rapidly closing in on him from all sides. D.C. found himself sympathizing with them. They had every right to. He wasn't one of them. He was something else. He couldn't become a werewolf like they were. He only partly resembled a human. His heart beat rapidly and a rage took him over. He wasn't angry with the pack. He was angry with himself. D.C. was angry with the fact that he was ever born.

D.C.'s whole body shuddered. Birth, was the mess of being born. There wasn't anything beautiful about the way a lamb had been squeezed out into this world. It was icky and slimy and quite frankly…disgusting. D.C. had been present at many births of livestock in the last year. Whenever he could, he'd not be found when the event was taking place. Thinking of it now made him want to hurl what contents he may have had his stomach.

D.C. turned his thoughts back towards his own creation. He thought he remembered being in the womb. It was warm yet cold all at the same time. Could it have been possible it was winter on the outside? He remembered his mother's musings as he lay sleepy inside of her uterus. Then all he could remember are screams and darkness. He remembered attempting to fight. He wanted to help her in her distress, but could not leave this dark place. It started to close in on him tightly. Grabbing, punching and clawing was all he was able to do. He felt her heartbeat grow weaker and he raged, even then, in the womb and lost control. He always lost control. D.C. never kept his composure when angry. He also lost his memories in the chaos.

D.C. stopped to sniff the air. He had to give himself a direction. This was an odd piece of advice when he thought about it. What direction can a murderer take that doesn't lead to more destruction? Why was it that he thrived on such anarchy? D.C. grunted. He had no idea or reasoning to lead him to any sort of a logical conclusion.

A distant howl broke his head trip. He snuffed the air through the rain. It was the pack. Another howl broke out. This time the calls had become a little louder. It sounded about a mile away at the most. D.C.'s heart began to pound harder in his chest. They were on his trail. He had to go. He could not allow them to kill him. Not until he had redeemed himself. He had to pay the price for his crime by making amends first. He didn't know why this was so important; he just knew that it was justice for his doing evil to allow his spirit to be freed. The problem was...where was he to go? How was he supposed to succeed in his task?

For the moment he decided just to run. The ground was soft as he entangled his path to weave through the leaves and sticks on the forest floor. Mud covered his feet, squished between his toes and engulfed his claws. He didn't want to leave prints if it could be helped, so where he could he would leap over shallow shrubs as well as level ground. His legs were strong and the distance fair considering the unfamiliar and uneven terrain of the ground. When a tree bough hung low enough he would raise one of his exceptionally long arms and grab hold of it. Lifting his feet he would swing himself as far as he could with the occasional ability to catch another branch before touching the ground again. He was attempting to not leave any of his sent behind so that it could be followed, at least not on the ground.

D.C. had also removed all of his clothes to attempt to throw them off his trail. He flung them as far as he could into the surrounding woods a few miles back. It did work for a moment, but not long enough for him to gain any real distance. He had to think of something better.

The Weres that followed him were much larger than him and looked very different. D.C. knew he was moving faster than the pack. He had some virtues after all, he surmised, speed being one of them. Unfortunately, he knew they had numbers and he was alone. They would eventually catch up, over power and kill him.

He stopped once he reached the bank of a river. Quickly he remembered Clive complaining when hunting how the hounds would lose the sent when they came upon water and it would sometime seem like forever for the dogs to pick it up again. The fact that he now stood on a bank of a river was a wonderful blessing. "Maybe someone is looking after me," D.C. thought to himself as he watched the rapidly running waters gush past.

Not knowing maps, D.C. couldn't identify what river it was. He did see the water flowed towards south east. D.C. bent down and picked up several rocks from the river's edge.

Haste was on his mind as he rubbed them against his body to cover them with his odor. He then threw them across the river with great force watching them land a good distance into the woods on the other side of the river. He had to gain distance. This was important. He needed to fool the pack into going the wrong direction. Another round of howls rang out. D.C. listened closely. They weren't even a half mile away and he thought he could see movement through the tree tops of their encroachment as they disturbed the trees and wildlife. He had gained some distance, but waiting in one spot wasn't smart.

D.C. shrugged his shoulders and jumped into the river. The water would not only carry him away from this spot, possibly more quickly than he was able to run, but would mask his scent as well. With a little luck, they would catch the scent on the rocks he had thrown and the hunters would make their way across the river and make their way north bound before realizing he had tricked them.

The icy spring rapids stung like a thousand whips against his skin. Even through his fur he felt their clips. There were still bits of ice in the water. D.C. half swam and half floated. He didn't even attempt to battle against the current. The water swept him into the center of the river. His entire body bobbed up and down through the waves. As water filled and cleared from his ears he noticed that there were no more hunting howls from the pack. It seemed that his trick had worked. Either that or he was being swept along with the water more quickly than he had anticipated. The current was growing faster, he came to notice. D.C. knew that this meant the river descended further downhill. He began to use his arms and legs to swim. The motions of his limbs were sure-enough, but as they had grown so numb from the frigid waters, he had little control.

D.C. fought against the current. "I waited too long," he scolded himself. Hypothermia was settling into his body. He strained harder to get his limbs functioning. Progress towards the far bank from which he had entered the river was happening, but slowly. He started humping his body as well. His limbs stroked in a single direction. He had no care as to where he landed on the bank. He just needed to land.

D.C.'s struggles had him finally reach the edge of the river after several failed attempts. Just as he lifted his right hand to grasp the soil on the edge of the water, he found himself digging his claws into the ground for a better grip. When he thought he had his bearings, a large chunk of drift wood rammed him in the shoulder blade and spun around, connecting to the back of his head as well. D.C. let out some sort of sound at the gash the log had made in his shoulder and possibly onto his head.

He reached, unthinking, toward the wound, letting go of the meager grip he had on the river's edge. The waters lapped at him with endless licks as he struggled once more to grab the river bank. That is when a larger piece of drift wood rammed him in the head again, causing him to yelp and swallow some of the water that was at the edge of his lips. D.C. wondered if drowning was how he was going to leave this world when the chunk of an antler from a deer stabbed him in the side just enough for him to lose his grip on the bank that he had just grabbed onto and sweep him into the rapid flow of the undertow.

D.C. held his breath as he tried to swim to the water's surface. He was so exhausted. He was unsure if the cause of his sudden tiredness was from the frigid spring waters, the onset of hypothermia or from the race to escape his hunters. In any case, he wasn't aware of his surroundings when the next piece of drift wood hit him bluntly in the left temple causing his head to swirl into darkness.

There was no saving him now, he thought. He was going to drown in the icy waters of whatever this river was and from what he could tell, his last coherent thought was, "I hate the dark."

Chapter 2

The morning sun was up over the trees that stood just beyond the clearing. It warmed the land and the skin on Sharon Miller's face. She was carrying an old tackle box and fishing pole as she walked along side of her nine year old son Jeremy. She promised him that they would go to the river and see if they could catch some fish in the early May waters.

Secretly, Sharon hoped they would catch enough to add to the freezer. Since the death of her husband just over a year earlier, running the farm had gotten a lot harder. He left them in some jam of a debt and not just with the bank. He also had taken out a substantial personal loan against the farm and it was all she could do to keep the creditors at bay. Mr. Robert

Doulson seemed to be an understanding and generous man, who was always firm when he spoke. Often, in the past year he offered to take the farm "off her hands" and give her some startup money to go somewhere new. She always refused, reminding him that it wasn't going anywhere. She wanted the place for her son. Doulson would nod without any further expression and simply say, "Thank you for the payment, this makes our transaction done for now."

Sharon was often left to wonder about that loan. She often felt that he was attempting to get her off the land and really didn't care about the money owing. She even went as far as asking her friend who worked for a lawyer in town if there was a reason her farm could be valuable. Maybe it was possible he wanted it so badly because it was sitting on a deposit of oil or gold. Her friend found out that it appeared to be just a piece of land. Sharon clenched her jaw. That was the only home her son had ever known and she would be damned to let it go.

Jeremy leaped and bounced along the grass toward the river in front of his mother. The short for his age, blond boy carried a bucket and collected the dew worms he saw squiggling on the top of the grass. This is how he and his dad would go fishing. Seeing a large worm he bent down to pick it up. Dangling it in front of his eyes he rolled it around in his fingers for a moment before dropping it into the bucket.

"Seventeen!" Jeremy happily shouted out to his mother.

She smiled at him. He was walking forward, looking back at her and smiling. Then, just as suddenly, he disappeared. He had tripped and fallen.

"Mom!" he cried out. This bellow sounded a bit strangled.

Sharon shook her head. The boy was clumsy. It was like his feet were too big for his legs to control. She smiled a little at this thought.

"Mom!" he hollered again, but this time more urgently.

Sharon stopped briefly and realized he hadn't picked himself back up. Panic hit her. Only her son could trip over his own two feet and break his leg! Without thought she dropped the tackle box and the rod and ran towards her injured offspring.

Upon arriving where Jeremy had

gone down, Sharon saw that her son was unbroken. She wasn't so sure about the heap of a hairy man that laid on the shoreline of the river.

- - - -

D.C.'s nostrils twitched as the smells of coffee, bacon and eggs worked their way up his nose. His eyes fluttered and opened. Everything was blurry at first. Then, as things worked their way into focus, he could see the old fireplace with red brick in front of him. It appeared to be on an odd angle and that's when D.C. concluded he was laying down.

His limbs were still numb and heavy with sleep. He closed his mouth and lifted his hand to wipe away the string of drool that had been attached to the puddle, spilled by him during his sleep. Groaning slightly, D.C. lifted himself into a sitting position. This is when his head started to throb. D.C. took his left hand and scratched it all over his shaggy head full of hair and then his pointed ear. He just felt itchy.

Looking around, he saw he was wearing some old grey track pants, a lumberjack's heavy wool plaid shirt and had been covered in what smelled like a goose down comforter. D.C. remembered that he had been naked when he had dove into the river. Now, he was sitting on a couch. The sofa was the kind with a wood frame and cushions. The pattern was of cottages at night along a creek somewhere in the woods. It was ugly.

The clank of a metal spoon on the edge of a pan forced D.C. to look to his right. A woman, in her late thirties was busy at her stove. It wasn't an old wood cook stove like he had been raised with at the farm house. It was all white, shiny and had blue flames under the fry pan. The room around it looked older than the stove did, except maybe the flowered wall paper. It was uglier than the couch.

As for the woman, she was dressed oddly too compared to Mildred who helped raise him at the farm. Her hair wasn't all white or in a bun. Instead it was brown and hung onto her shoulders. Her skin was smooth, clear and pink. It had not spotted or wrinkled. She wore jeans and a t-shirt. Also, she wasn't wearing an apron which explained why when the egg crackled and spit grease all over her shirt she whispered, "Shit!" dropped the spatula and grabbed a cloth to wipe away the spot. Of course, this only made the spot show up more and spread itself into the fabric of the shirt.

"Mom," a young male voice creaked, "he's up!" This is when D.C. saw the youngster sitting at the table, furthest from him. His eyes were wide with wonder as they stared in D.C.'s direction. D.C. didn't think the kid could blink his eyes were so big.

The woman stopped rubbing at the grease spot on her shirt, stood up straight, and looked in three or four different directions before making eye contact with her house guest. She put on a slight, shy smile. Her pheromones told D.C. she was nervous.

"Hi there," she finally said. "I'm glad to see you're awake. I hope you're okay and all."

D.C. wasn't sure what to make of all this so he just nodded. Instinct forced him to be cautious.

She smiled again, this time wider. She backed herself away from the stove and moved towards him a little. Caution was in her demeanor. D.C. could relate to this behavior. "My son and I went fishing, early, just after sun up and we found you were laying on the bank of the river about four or five miles west of here. I wasn't sure if you were hurt."

D.C. looked past her at the fair haired boy and then down at his clothes.

"You were kind of awake, I don't know if you remember, but you used Jeremy and I like crutches until we got you into the house and on the couch," she explained. "You've only been asleep for about an hour. Don't feel you have to get up or nothing." She was wringing her hands a little when she said the last sentence.

D.C. picked at the sleeve of his shirt.

"You weren't wearing' anything," she said. "I dressed you in clothes that belonged to my late husband. I hope they're okay. You're not as big as he was," she offered. "but with your hair and, " he eyes briefly gazed towards his crotch before she turned slightly pink and turned to look towards her son, "all I thought you may not mind the loose fit until we figured out who you are and where you're from."

D.C. nodded his head. It wasn't the first time he had shown up out of the blue, naked and unconscious. In fact, that's how he was when he arrived at the old farm about a year ago, when Clive found him, naked, unconscious and laying in hay stack. This could turn into a bad habit, he thought to himself.

The woman suddenly smiled wide again and shook her head. "I'm sorry, I forgot my manners." She licked her lips and held out her right hand as she moved towards him. "My name is Sharon Miller."

D.C. looked at her hand. He wasn't sure what he was supposed to do. His name was Death Cub. The old farmer, after teaching him English and learning what his real name was had decided it should be shortened to D.C.. Clive had explained it made himself and his wife feel more comfortable. After learning the meaning of his name with an English translation, D.C. felt no need to argue the "nickname". As for a last name, he didn't have one. Clive and Mildred only ever introduced him to a handful of others, mostly other farmers and only ever men and when they did it was always, "This is our farm hand, D.C."

D.C. crinkled up his long nose as he contemplated the hand of Sharon Miller. Should he tell her his proper name was Death Cub or D.C.? What about a last name? He closed his eyes. He was smart and had to think fast. He could see she was growing more worried about the man who sat on her couch and remained silent while ignoring her friendly hand shake.

In a moment that felt like forever, D.C.'s mind took him back to the day the old farmer, Clive Hill, found him snuggled into the hay out in the field. The sun was bright and he woke only slightly when the farmer placed a hand on his shoulder. The concern on the old man's face was genuine. Words, flowing like music were spouted by the old man's mouth even though D.C. didn't understand a word. The man helped D.C. out of the hay that morning and into his life. Before that moment, there was only dark accompanied by shadows, ghost and monsters.

To Sharon, it appeared D.C. was just about to grab her hand when he spoke. His voice, abstractly deep for such a slim man, but somehow suited him with his odd appearance quietly introduced himself, "Hayes. D.C. Hayes."

Sharon sighed in relief and retracted her hand. It was obvious that D.C. had no desire to touch her. Fidgeting a little she directed D.C.'s attention back to the fair haired boy at the table. "This is my son, Jeremy."

D.C. gave a single nod of the head. He wanted to attempt a smile to show he had no ill will towards them, but the two rows of sharp teeth prevented him from doing so. He thought he could try a closed mouth smile. Mildred had him practice those frequently so that he didn't have to show his teeth, but D.C. never felt his smile was something anyone wanted to see.

"Please, come join us for breakfast. I know it's almost noon, but we're all getting a late start to the day."

D.C. stood and looked towards the table. A true breakfast as he knew it was laid out; bacon, eggs, milk, orange juice and even grits. He wondered...will this now be home?

Chapter 3

After breakfast D.C. politely and quietly helped Sharon with the dishes. He dried them as she washed them. Jeremy watched with curiosity about this strange man in his father's clothes. They were just past cleaning the silverware when Jeremy's first question came rapidly from his lips, "Are you a werewolf?"

Aghast by his inquiry his mother half laughed at the question purposed and half out of embarrassment. "Jeremy!" she scolded sharply, "What kind of a question is that?"

Jeremy shrugged his shoulders, "I dunno. Just his covered in hair and I've heard that people covered in hair are werewolves."

D.C. just looked towards the boy. The pup didn't know any better and the old man on the farm had a word he used when people came visiting to describe D.C. and his odd appearance.

"Hypertichosis," D.C. stated just a bit louder than a whisper. He wasn't truly answering the boy as he was practicing the old farmer's word.

"Hyper-trick-o-is?" Jeremy repeated with a puzzled sound.

D.C. broke away from his thoughts of Clive. More clearly he spoke with his deep voice, "It means excessive hair. It's a rare condition." He turned back to the dishes. "Werewolves don't exist." was his last statement as he picked up a dinner plate with his left hand to dry it with the towel in his right. D.C. wasn't so sure about that last statement. The beasts that hunted him looked a lot like werewolves to him. Not to mention the large, black ghost wolf he thought he saw the night he had been chased by it into the haystack on Clive Hill's farm.

Seeing how uncomfortable D.C. had become, Sharon looked towards her son, "Why don't you go play outside."

"Okay," he replied happily running towards the screen door and out to the yard. Jeremy screeched a little as he went and even louder once he got into the old tire swing hanging from the willow in the yard.

Sharon sighed. "I'm sorry."

D.C. nodded. His silence wasn't out of upset. Children ask questions.

Often they ask inappropriate ones. It was just hard lying to the boy about what he was. He *was* a "werewolf" of sorts. He had come to that conclusion over the past year while living on the farm. D.C. just wasn't a very good one. He hoped repaying the powers that be for lying to the boy wasn't going to be as complicated or as hard as it was going to be for the murder he knew he would or had already committed.

Just like that the vision of the dead wolf flooded his thoughts. She laid there, lifeless, her spine twisted and broken. Her insides spilled to the outside. D.C. could see her eyes. They were fixed, cold and glaring. She was dead yet able to still judge him for his crime against her. Then, he saw the shadow of the black wolf jump out at him and snarl. This brought D.C. back to the kitchen where he was drying dishes beside Sharon. He let out a gasp of relief. He hadn't dropped the plate he was drying. The only relief in the matter of the murder was that he could see in his visions the face of the victim. Sharon was not her. He knew he was safe around her.

Sharon found the man drying her dishes oddly quiet. She didn't think he was around here to cause any harm. She was more frightened of Doulson and his constant jabber than she was of this strange fellow. She glanced at him once or twice trying not to stare. He was definitely an odd one. It wasn't just the excessive hair all over his body. It was his pointed ears, long nose, and square jaw that jutted out from the rest of his face. Sharon thought for a moment that maybe her son was right. Maybe this man was a "werewolf". She stared into the dishwater and at her pruning fingers.

Letting out a sigh she dismissed the thought again. D.C. had most likely told her the honest truth about that trick thing he had. Still...she was going to look it up on the internet as soon as she got to the library in town.

They quietly finished the dishes. Sharon then invited D.C. to try on an old pair of her husband's shoes and to sit on the porch of the farm house. Sharon took a tray of lemonade out to the porch as D.C. stopped to look at the lineup of shoes and boots that had been her mate's. They were all neatly arranged. No dust. Maybe it hasn't been long since he passed.

D.C. wondered if the farm with Clive and his wife, Mildred would now just collect dust. He knew they were gone. The pack wouldn't allow them to live. Not for harboring a fugitive like himself. D.C. had seen enough of those mob movies to know that this was true. Still he wondered about the pair; if they were okay. After all, the pack descended on him while he was doing chores in the barn, a long way from the house where Clive and Mildred would be resting after a meal.

The ghost wolf showed up first, nipping at his heels making him run. He heard the pack shortly after. He didn't think they had even gone near the house. Maybe he should go back and check on them. D.C. blinked a couple of times, to prevent tears from falling. He knew he couldn't go back. They would have a century there waiting no matter how long it was. He bet that even after he was dead there would be someone there waiting in case his spirit should happen to stop by. He had to put the elderly couple out of his mind and into his past. With no way to repay them for their generosity and kindness he didn't want to bring them heartache or strife. If the pack had let them be, they would just think he had moved along. He was full grown to their knowledge and even though D.C. was with them a long time, he had heard Clive and the other farmers talk about their help leaving frequently to look for better work or more pay somewhere else.

D.C. turned his thoughts back to the footwear. He didn't like footwear or socks. The claws on his feet always tore through the fabric within a day and the shoe within the week. Besides, both made his feet itch. He decided to go out to the porch without anything on his feet. He hoped Sharon wasn't going to be offended.

Chapter 4

D.C. sat in the chair on the opposite side of the small table where Sharon put down the pitcher of lemonade and glasses. He stared out at the yard with the sprouting hay and could just see the red painted wood of the barn sticking up out of the field. Once the hay had reached full height, the barn wouldn't be visible from the porch at all.

As Sharon handed him a glass of lemonade he noticed she was staring at his bare feet. D.C. could almost hear her thoughts. He looked down at his feet. They were covered in heavy fur on top, bare and black from walking in the dirt on the bottom and he didn't have toenails. He had hard, thick, curved claws just like on his fingers.

"I don't like shoes," D.C. stated with some annoyance in Sharron's stare. He then quickly wished he hadn't said anything at all. He could see that her stare was more wonder than irritation.

She shook her head slightly as if coming out of a trance and looked up into his face. "Where are you from?" she ventured to ask. "You were...well...naked. Should I call someone one for you?" Her concern was genuine. D.C. could see and smell it.

D.C. looked down into his glass of lemonade. "No one to call," he bluntly told her. He wished he could have her call Clive and let them know he was alright. That would be stupid though. He didn't need the hunting party finding him here.

"Well...then Mr. Hayes," Sharon said lifting her glass to her lips to have a drink. "If you need shelter and a job, I really could use a farm hand."

D.C. continued to stare into his drink. He lived on a farm since he could remember. When the old farmer, Clive, pulled him from the hay stack, he put D.C. in the barn until he learned English and could be respectable as a house guest and not an animal. D.C. liked the thought of staying here, but wasn't sure it was such a good idea. Maybe he could stay, for just a bit. If he could get himself some cash together he might be able to take a bus or something out of the area. He had heard from Mildred that the mountains in a place called Colorado were beautiful. He could see himself as a mountain man. The cold really didn't bother him, at least, not much.

D.C. raised his head and looked back towards the barn. He could see that Sharon was watching Jeremy play with a stick by the willow, but she was anxiously awaiting an answer from him.

"I'll stay in the barn," D.C. said as he finally took a swig of lemonade. He gritted his teeth and tried not to flinch at the sour flavor of the beverage. He never really liked it. He always drank it as it seemed to be customary and polite to do so.

"The barn!" Sharon exclaimed. "I have extra room in the house..."

"The barn," D.C. stated firmly as he finished his glass of juice. He looked her straight in the eyes. His golden eyes held her firmly in their gaze. Sharon found herself a little frightened and excited at the same time.

D.C. stood up and walked himself off the porch and across the field to the barn. If his hunters were to locate him here, he wanted it to be out there. That way, he could claim with dying breath that he was hiding out without Sharon's knowledge.

Jeremy watched as D.C. distinctive walk lead him past the willow where he was playing with his stick. Curious he looked at his mom on the porch. He hadn't heard what had transpired. Jeremy grinned and went back to his game of poking things with his stick. Everything was more interesting when you poked it with a stick.

Sharon was sitting there with her arms folded across her chest and staring off across the field after D.C.'s wake. He was odd. She felt that he had been through some sort of trauma.

She just hoped it wasn't going to throw any more bad luck her way.

The boy ran up onto the porch and flopped into the chair D.C. had shortly occupied across from his mother. "Is he leaving mom?" the boy asked excitedly. "I don't want him to go."

Sharon broke her gaze on D.C. to look at her son. "No, he's just going to the barn." She didn't want to comment any further. She had no further comment. She wasn't sure what she should think just now.

They both looked back over the field of hay and D.C. was nowhere to be seen.

Chapter 5

Dreams saturated D.C.'s brain as he slept in the loft of the barn. It didn't take long for exhaustion to take his body over and even less time for the fragments of images to parade through his mind.

Inside his head D.C. was in a dark wooded area. He recognized it as the woods he ran through just the night before. He could hear the howling again of his hunters. D.C. felt his heart begin to race and the adrenalin run through his body. He began to run. As his feet hit the ground it was like a slow motion that his foot would hit the dirt, curl up scraping his large clawed nails on the ground. The motion was making him almost fly for a moment. As the river came into sight a grotesque smell invaded his nostrils. Part of it smelled like decaying flesh and part of it smelled of burning rope or grass. At the river's edge he could see it flowed true and clear. D.C. looked into the waters. Staring back at him was a large, black wolf with yellow eyes. It was the ghost that chased him the first night out of the woods and had stalked him ever since. The wolf seemed to be trying to tell him something, but it was all in yips and growls that D.C. could not understand. Suddenly the waters turned murky, like a milk glass that was to be rinsed. The river also seemed to become solid. D.C. backed away as it coiled itself up and turned its monstrous head to stare at D.C.. It was clearly the worm, Leviathan. Mildred had told him of this monster in her bible teachings as he was learning to read, speak and write. The worm screamed as it opened its mouth, showing the rows of sharpened teeth to

D.C. as it struck out like a snake to devour him.

D.C. choked back a scream as his eyes flared open and he found himself in a sitting position, his heart still pounding firmly against his chest and the screech of the worm still ringing in his ears. He closed his eyes and took in a deep breath. He could still smell the burning of grass in the air. His eyelids flickered. He opened them and ran toward the window. It wasn't a dream. The hayfield was burning.

- - - -

Sharon had seen the Lexus drive up the way towards the house. She didn't think much of it. Another payment to Mr. Doulson was due and here he came, right on cue, one hour after sun down.

Sharon walked over to stand beside Jeremy who was sitting at the table working on some homework. She leaned over his shoulder and stroked his hair with her left hand. Quietly she watched for him a moment. "Time to put the books away," she told him. "You've had a long day and tomorrow is Sunday so there's time to finish then."

"Okay mom," he answered as he put his pencil down and started closing up the books and neatly piling them on the table.

"Thank you," Sharon said to him as she looked out the window.

The car was directly outside and four large men were climbing out. No

Mr. Doulson this time from what she could see. She walked over to the cupboard above the stove and grabbed the envelope filled with five hundred dollars, all in small bills. It was only about half of what she should be paying him, but she sold the last thing she had of any value last week when Jeremy had gotten sick and she suddenly had to pay for a prescription.

Looking in the envelope briefly she attempted to swallow her tears. She hated this. She worked double shifts at a cruddy diner that forced her to wear the blouse a little too low cut and her skirt a little too short so she could get better tips. Her wages went to lining the pockets of the bank and her tips went to line the pockets of this Mr. Doulson. She knew when her late husband had borrowed the money it could get paid back quickly, as it was just supposed to be a small loan so they could run the farm for the season. As it turned out, her husband died and the debt fell onto her shoulders.

The door to the farm house flew open. Sharon, startled out of her thought began to yell, "What are you doing?"

One large man with a square jaw closed in towards her while two of the others snatched up her son.

"Mommy!" Jeremy called out terrified.

"Nate! Put my boy down!" Sharon scolded. Her anger rose above her fear.

The man who was closest to her spoke. "Sorry, ma'am. We've got to follow orders." Just like that, Sharon could not react to the club that was striking her across her head and causing her to fall to the floor. She was hit a second time on the other side of her head once she had landed. Helpless, she could see her son struggle against the men. Her view became obstructed as a third whack connected to her forehead. Her eyes blurred and couldn't remain open. The envelope of money parted from her hand and slid gently onto the floor. She tried to lift herself up. It was futile. Sharon Miller was down for the count.

- - - -

Rapidly, D.C. launched himself into a full run and leapt from the loft onto the barn floor. Faster than eyes could see he burst through the barn door and into the field. At a blink of an eye he was alongside the farmhouse and grabbing the hose and turning on the water. He returned to the field and cursed as his own acceleration was faster than the water. The hay shoots were igniting one off the other in a chain. A dry spring with little rain was leaving the land in drought. The only good thing was that it had only just sprouted and was low to the ground.

D.C. thought quickly. He dropped the hose and began to run, purposely kicking up dirt to smother the flames. Around the perimeter he went until the circle grew smaller and smaller. The dirt was choking the fire by depriving it of oxygen. Just as he ran out of energy he stepped on the last ember in the grass.

D.C. paused to look at the damage. Even in the dim light of a waxing moon he could clearly see that his efforts had kept the damage to a confined area. With a quick till and reseeding the hay could recover its growth and be cut on time with the rest of the field. Clive would be proud that D.C. had listened so closely to his farming lessons.

D.C. walked over the hose that was sputtering water. He bent down and picked it up slowly. That's when he heard the scream from the house. He looked up at the dwelling when he heard Sharon scream a second time.

- - - -

Before D.C. had woken from his sleep in the barn, the four henchmen of Robert Doulson bound and gagged Jeremy to put him into the car. The boy had a cut on his head. He had struggled and fought to escape. During the melee in the kitchen his head jerked and banged against the edge of the table, slicing it open. The wound really was only a scratch, but bled profusely, leaving blood trailing.

Jeremy was placed in the backseat. The driver hadn't gotten in yet. He cried and whimpered as loudly as he could. The police officer who had come to his school had told his class that if they were in danger, sometimes crying played on the sympathy of their captor to let their victim go. His cries were falling on deaf ears. The three men in the car were too busy bantering among themselves.

"What's he doin'?" asked the one Sharon had referred to as "Nate" from the back seat of the car.

The other in the back seat shrugged his shoulders. "Knowing him, he's probably adding a finishing touch. If he doesn't get to kill something he gets all uptight."

Jeremy stared at the words that flowed from the large man in the grey suit and light hair. He cried louder. He was scared even more now. There was someone who wanted to kill in this group! Tears streamed endlessly from his eyes.

The driver door opened and the fourth climbed in. Closing the door he adjusted his position. He then started the car and began to drive off.

"What were you doing?" The man in the front passenger seat asked. "You know the boss gave us strict orders."

The driver grinned from ear to ear before he answered. "Boss said he wants the land."

The other three men looked at each other. Jeremy tried to cry louder. The driver waited with excitement for the unsaid question.

Finally, the light haired one in the back seat spoke, "Okay...I'll bite. What do you mean by that?"

Almost jumping in the seat the driver reasoned out an explanation. "The boss wants the land. Well...if there's nothing on the land it'll be that much easier. I set the field on fire. I figure with the old dried out barn and house it'll get a good wildfire going. That'll kill off the crop and that bitch's spirit." He then laughed at the great joke he felt he accomplished.

The others just listened to his laughter, not really getting the humor to the situation. Jeremy stopped his wailing. He realized his tears weren't working. The whole car fell into silence after about a minute as it raced down the old dirt roads of the country.

Chapter 6

Taking no time to think or caution to what could be happening within the house, D.C. dropped the spurting hose and took off, barreling toward the house. He was sure his claws scratched the wooden rise as he pushed the door open and entered the kitchen. The smell of garbage mingled with the smell of fresh blood in the air. This room was no longer warm. It felt cold and offensive to his inner nature.

Crumpled on the floor was Sharon, distraught. She squeezed her night dress closed with one hand and clutched a piece of paper tightly with the other. Red droplets could be seen on the table and the floor. D.C. forced himself to breathe in deeply. The place smelled of a horrible rot and blood.

The droplets were blood, from Jeremy, the boy. They were small, but splattered seemingly everywhere. D.C. looked closer with his eyes. He was able to deduce that it was a small injury the boy was suffering from. There would be much more blood had it been anything more.

D.C. moved into the kitchen as his hackles rose, edging himself towards Sharon. He wasn't sure that whoever it was that had been here was gone. Their scent was so over powering.

Suddenly realizing D.C.'s presence, Sharon looked up into his face. "They took Jeremy," she said shaking. Her eyes had become swollen with tears and her forehead had a large bruise beginning to show. She let go of her nightdress and flattened out the crumpled letter. "They say if I call the police that they will kill him." She tried handing the letter to D.C., but her grip failed and the page fluttered its way to the floor.

Sharon buried her head in her hands and began to wail. She was having a hard time grasping the reality of the events that had transpired not even half an hour ago.

D.C.'s eyes narrowed as he bent down to his knees, towards the letter. He wasn't letting his guard down. The perpetrators that had been here prior to his arrival had an evil that left a stench in the air that could only be compared to a decomposing corpse. He used only his fingertips under his long clawed nails to pick the letter up. First he bent his head towards the letter and inhaled. D.C. snuffed, shook his head wildly for a moment and choked down the urge to become angered about the scent. He knew he had to keep his mind clear. An innocent was in danger. An innocent not like him.

D.C. then looked at the markings on the letter. They had a strange slant and curled together. He never had seen writing like this. Mildred was teaching him to read and write the words they spoke, but D.C. figured himself ignorant as he never read fast and often forgot the meaning behind "printed letters" as Mildred would call them. The markings on the paper sort of resembled these letters, but more flowery. D.C. remembered briefly at that moment when Clive or Mildred wrote something down and it wasn't for his teachings, that their writing looked similar to this.

D.C. looked up from the paper. Sharon was staring at him. Her crying had subsided for the moment. Her eyes where wet and red rimmed. Her nose was running and she didn't clean it up. She just stared at D.C..

"Read it to me," he stated as he shoved the paper into her hands. "I don't know how to identify these markings."

Taken a little aback, Sharon nodded her head and began to read the letter:

"Miss Miller. Although your efforts to repay your husband's debts have been admirable I am afraid it is not enough. Sign the deed to your farm to me and get off the land and I will see that as even to our debt. I have made this request of you in the past. I'm no longer willing to negotiate. To prove my sincerity I have taken your son. Don't involve the law or I will find my way to making sure the boy is never seen alive again. You will

*come to the Mill Cafe in Fort Hunt the day
after tomorrow. Noon sharp. The deed will
be ready for you to sign and then I'll tell you
where to pick up the boy. I suggest you take
the time to remove any personal belonging from
the property as you will not be permitted to
return. Thank you for doing business.*

Robert Doulson."

She let her hands rest from holding the paper. To her it felt like it weighed a thousand pounds. The words she read aloud sunk into her head a little deeper this time than they had the first time she read them only minutes earlier.

D.C. looked at her. She looked at him and found herself lost in his yellow eyes. "Stay here. Clean up. Don't let on to anyone anything has gone on."

Sharon gave D.C. a puzzled look. Then she got angry. "This bastard has taken my son! What do you mean by telling me to relax and clean and pretend?" She was shouting her words at the end, mixing them with new tears and frenzy.

D.C. bared his teeth. Sharon hunched herself up. Seeing him like this suddenly caused her to quiet down. This man really was some sort of a monster. She was now sure of it. Regrettably, this was the only other being out there who knew and was appearing to help her now. She straighten her back, finally wiped her nose on the sleeve of her nightdress and looked fiercely into his matching gaze. She was going to show him that she was strong and he would not be able to prey on her.

D.C. could see he had her attention. He liked how she went from soft to hard so quickly. He took this moment in and spoke clearly so she wouldn't misunderstand. "I will retrieve your offspring and you will be staying here. It is my calling for reasons I cannot go into right now. Stay inside and don't let on to anyone anything has happened. If I haven't returned your boy by the morning after next then do as the letter says because I'm dead."

Sharon was without words. The slight nod from her head was instinct more than acknowledgment that she understood every word D.C. had just said. Shock was settling into her body. She was becoming numb.

D.C. stood up. It was clear that they were the only ones in the house. With any luck, the kidnappers that had been here didn't know he was even on the property. That could only work to his advantage.

D.C. walked out of the door and onto the porch. He had no idea what he was going to do. Something in his blood was driving him to do it. Instead of staying calm now he allowed the smell of *bane* course through his veins. His eyes glowed with a brighter yellow and he let out a howl signaling the hunt. He thought he could hear the howl returned to him from somewhere else. He also thought he could see the shadow of the ghost wolf creep up next to him within his own shadow. It was not time to chase or be chased by shadows.

Before Sharon could pick herself up and go to the door after hearing D.C.'s battle cry, the strange man her son found naked next to the river was gone. The only sign of his presence

were the odd scrapes on the door
passage floor and the garden hose
running in the field.

Chapter 7

D.C. was being guided by the scent of the filth in his nostrils; the rage of his anger pumping through his veins. He wasn't really seeing where he was heading even though his eyesight was sharp. He was fueling himself on instinct. The adrenalin that coursed through him came from an endless tap.

His mind relaxed as he washed away into his fever. Flashes from his dream in the barn came to his mind as he tangled himself through the countryside. The giant black wolf could be felt growling and nipping at his heels. D.C. didn't have to look to know it was at his heels again. He was left confused by this. The hunters that hunted him down spoke like this. They were his enemies, but in the dream it was the giant worm that was his foe, not the wolf. Could it be that the wolf was actually an ally?

D.C. suddenly came to a halt. Dust and dirt came loose from the ground with the abrupt stop. The wind had changed. The scent drifted off the roadway. He was going to have to search for which way they went. They must have gone down wind now, he thought to himself.

D.C. dropped to his knees. Putting his nose to the ground, he had to smell for fresh exhaust from their vehicle. He even was groping for the slight residue of rubber that would be left by their car tires. The dogs on the farm showed him how to track in this manner and he knew they had good noses. Clive used them to track down stray cattle and deer.

"Dog". D.C. jolted his upper

body upright. One hunter, who saw him in the hay, was growling and yipping. Clearly he became aware that it had said the word, "Dog," as a referral to him. D.C. allowed his mind to rest and his eyes grew bigger. The growls, yips and barks were their language. The giant wolf in his dream was speaking. D.C. now viewed the beast as a "*dog*". This may not be the most accurate description of his specter, but it was more accurate than any other interpretation he could come up with.

Angry with himself for not being intelligent enough to have figured out all this sooner, D.C.'s rage took over. He pressed his nose against the ground with his teeth bared and hackles up. He could feel his body grow stronger. His legs lengthen. His claws turn into talons. All of his senses become more acute. He was expanding and changing, not just in the head either, but his whole body.

Breathing in deeply he caught the scent of the worm. He envisioned its horrific maw opening to tear into him. The smell it belched out from the depths of its belly was identical to the one left at the Miller home. A separate flash of the giant wolf entered his head as a small howl. D.C. understood the word the daemon used. That word was "*bane*". Something deep inside of his being told him that this was something he was born to fight against. This *was* the thing that was going to lead him to his redemption for his crime.

D.C. bounded to his feet and with a screaming howl allowed himself to be on the hunt again; his body and mind transforming as he went. For the first time in his life D.C. was aware he had a purpose and a calling. He may be hunted, but now he was also a hunter.

There was a way to redeem himself and his fate.

D.C. sped even faster. It was time to embrace who he was. He was "Death Cub."

- - - -

The vehicle transporting the four kidnappers and the Miller boy had long since arrived at their destination. The driver, known as "Butcher" and the fair haired one from the back seat, known as "William", were sitting inside an old, moss covered cabin deep in the woods next to the river.

Jeremy had been carried in a fireman's lift into the cabin and shoved by the corner were an old wood stove used to sit. All there was were ashes and blackened floor boards. He was at least put into a sitting position and not left to be curled up. His hands and legs were tied together at the ankles and wrists. There was no way for the boy to attempt to stand up. His mouth was gagged by one of his mother's own tea towels. Jeremy couldn't help thinking that she was going to be very angry should he put a hole in it.

William stood by the window. Butcher had found himself a seat at the table with a glass of water.

"Do you think she's gonna go tell the police?" William asked. This was his first trip out on something like this and he had no idea what to expect.

Butcher smiled and grabbed the deck of cards to shuffle. "She's not stupid. How is she gonna explain to the police that she's been paying back an illegal debt for over a year that her dead husband left her."

William shrugged his shoulders and looked at the other man. "Witnesses turn state evidence all the time, even when they were up to their own necks in the conspiracy."

Butcher's grin grew wider. "Have a seat and let me explain something to you."

William frowned a little, but did what he was told. He may be unfamiliar with to this type of criminal behavior, but he wanted logical answers.

Butcher watched as the other man sat down on the chair across the table. Without looking at William at all he started dealing out the cards. He also started talking. "When you put the kid down over there I got a glass of water to put over here."

William looked confused. Butcher saw this and rolled his tongue in his cheek. He then sighed. "Think of this water as the mother of this kid. She wants to be with her baby. She needs to protect it. Therefore, if she wants to be united with the kid she gonna have to give us what we want."

"What Robert Doulson wants."

"Actually," Butcher interjected, "What your boss wants."

William shook his head. "Would it not just be easier to get rid of them both?"

Butcher laughed at his counterpart's statement. "I've met your boss and she has a little of me in her, that's for sure. I think she would just like to off them, but when she had Daniel Miller met with his little hunting accident last year, her boss sent out an inquiry to my boss; ever since they've had to be partners. He's scratching her back while she's scratching his."

William shook his head. He didn't understand a thing this guy was saying. It was all too twisted and he hadn't been around long enough to sort any of it out.

Butcher motioned to the messy stack of cards in front of William. "Pick them up." he said. "It's gonna be a long couple of days."

William reached out and cautiously examined the cards he was dealt. Looking at his hand he made a mental note of what was there; Ace of Spades, ten of Spades, Jack of Spades,

Queen of Spades and a two of hearts.

Butcher cursed as he looked at his own hand, "I got crap! How about you?"

"I think I'm digging myself a hole," was his quiet reply.

Chapter 8

The old wooden cottage blended well against its surroundings. It almost was invisible with the overgrowth of plants and moss on its sides. The babble of the river kept the noises from inside muted. If it wasn't for the fact that D.C.'s hearing was sharper than most animals, he may have missed Jeremy's whimpers coming from within the place. It was those little mews he had caught with his pointed ears that let him know that he was tracking the perpetrators correctly.

He ventured flat against the ground as he made his way closer to the building. He didn't want to risk being noticed. He also kept himself downwind in case they could smell his sweat that had beaded and burst across his skin and fur. Once reaching the foundation of the house he tilted his head to see more closely where it was he had crawled to. D.C. smiled inwardly. He was directly under a window. The light was faint from the slight opening in the drapes. He could hear lowered voices inside as well.

D.C. slowly raised his body from the ground until his head was level with the window's lower frame. Listening, he could make out the sounds of the boy's muffled crying as well as two deeper toned voices. He could also pick out a shuffling sound. It was the rubbing of playing cards being moved against each other. D.C. lowered himself back against the ground. He had to think. He had to act swiftly and give them no time to harm the child.

D.C. closed his eyes to concentrate. The sounds of the river filled his head. D.C. cursed to himself,

"If only the river would be quiet!"
That is when it seemed to grow louder.
D.C. opened his eyes and thought he
saw the giant wolf ghost standing on
the river bank. D.C. shook his head
wildly for a moment or two. This was
no time for his delusions. He looked
towards the river again. At that
moment he saw a man standing next to
the wolf. He was smaller than D.C.
and looked puny next to his ghost.
D.C. could not take his eyes off of the
strange figure and found himself
moving towards the river's edge.
Silently, they beckoned and called.
D.C. was compelled to answer.

Upon reaching the bank, D.C.
woke slightly from his trance and
thankfully realized he was still on his
belly on the ground. If he had stood
up, it would have exposed him for
sure. D.C. wasn't so sure that the men
in the cabin, the boy and his ghosts

were the only other ones out here this
night. He also witnessed that the man
and the wolf were gone. D.C. looked
into the water and into his own yellow
eyes inside of the reflection. He
thought he saw something, just for a
moment, inside the reflection of his iris
and pupil. His gaze into himself
became more intense.

Not knowing the source of this
magic, D.C. was pulled in and almost
felt drowned by the intensity of the
spell. He became incorporeal in a way,
feeling his body lay against the damp
grass of the river bank, but also drifting
listlessly on the wind.

With a blink of an eye, that
seemed to press slowly against
whatever time physically could be
construed as, D.C. was looking around
a small, dimly lit room. The walls were
worn out wooden planks, and he was

somewhere about the middle of the room. Everything was contorted. The edges of his sight seemed rounded, like a bubble. D.C. saw everything at one time. Nothing had a hard shape. D.C. had to fight for a focus. He looked around and immediately saw Jeremy. Whatever this spell was doing to his head, D.C. didn't begin to guess, but it was allowing him to see what he most desired.

The boy was huddled into a corner with his hands and feet tied together. There was a red piece of cloth tied around his mouth. A mark on the boy's left eyebrow was visible. It was crusted over now an ugly looking scab. This must have been where he was hit during his kidnapping.

D.C.'s eyes focused on something else. Much closer were two men, average in build sitting almost on top of where he was seeing? They were dressed casually and playing cards across the table. He could see the cards in the one's hand clearly. He had to look up to see faces as if he were dwarfed. As he looked, the image of the biting worm with his maw opened wide struck out at him from both faces.

D.C. jumped up from the bank and scurried to hide next to the building. He was finding his breath hard to catch. They were both this horrid worm that D.C. had in his nightmare. What was he to do now?

Chapter 9

Closing his eyes and taking in a deep breath, D.C. crouched against the back of the building. He had to find courage. He felt his own puffing breath escaping his mouth. It seemed to meet the breath of another. He opened his eyes and the giant, black ghost of a dog that had followed him in his dreams and in his life was staring at him face to face. He could feel the wolf's breath against his own.

D.C. froze. He didn't know what to do.

"Grarge pfft grrrr aine," came thundering low from the mouth. D.C.'s eyes widened and he finally blinked. He understood the words. The creature clearly said to him, "It is the Bane."

"What is Bane?" D.C. found himself asking the creature only to have it step away. From behind him was the man he saw on the bank a few moments earlier. This one with the antlers of a stag, proudly displayed on the top of his head. D.C. wondered if this man was part animal as well. He didn't remember such an elaborate headdress moments earlier when he had been drawn to the pair on the bank of the river.

"Death Cub, " he spoke clearly. "It is time for you to take your place among the Garu as a martyr and not a fugitive."

D.C. gulped an intake of air. He was as frightened by this one man as he was by a whole pack of werewolves. He couldn't move or speak.

"I ordained that this is to be," said the man. "The hunting pack for your head is on its way and when they see you fight with my son, Fenris," he pointed to the large wolf next to him, "they will realize that you are protected and looked after by the Great Loki and should not be harmed."

D.C. shut his eyes again. He had delusions before, but this one was taking the cake. D.C. looked head on into the face of the black wolf. Choking a little he found words, "You have haunted me all of my known life; awake or asleep. How am I to know that you are here to help, guide and protect me?"

Loki smiled as Fenris stepped closer and stared evenly into D.C.'s eyes. Using his Garu speech, that D.C. had quickly grasped and now understood the wolf responded, "I have not haunted you. I have watched over you. I am not a nightmare, but a loving dream. I did not chase you. I only aggressively showed you the way. I have kept watch over you. This was all done out of love, from a father to a motherless son. I did my part as your surviving parent."

D.C.'s mind broke and shattered. It then reassembled into a million pieces; an illogical mass of insightful musings.

- - - -

It was dark and warm where D.C. slept. He could feel a slight coolness through the walls of his room if he shifted himself ever so slightly.

He could hear the familiar tromp of a steady beat along with the rush of something all around him. He heard the yips and musings of an outside voice. It was soft and caring. It was comfortable where he was, for several weeks...

The quiet was shattered abruptly. The soft voice was raked into painful howls. His room was cramped and tightening. D.C. reacted. The thumping beat was irregular and the flow of other sounds cut off. He didn't like this. It hurt his Eden of where he was. He found himself raging against the atrocities that were seemingly surrounding him. He pounded his fists and kicked his legs at first. This was not accomplishing anything except to make the assault on his utopia worsen. He opened his eyes, there was only the dark. No light glow as he had seen from time to time. He became uncontrollable. His bones cracked. His body budged. He blindly used his claws and dug into the walls of his room, ripping them apart without care. He was going after the thing that was making him bezerk.

The cold breeze of the air hit him. He was wet and he was cold. A large glowing orb hung in the sky and rapidly ascended higher. D.C. stared at this object with detestation. He growled at it as it rose higher and loomed over him. He knew that this was the cause of his discomfort. Loathing the orb he saw. He knew there was going to be no way he could climb up and catch it. It had the power to pull on him and he was powerless.

D.C. sneered. He had torn his way through the gates of heaven to go after an intangible foe. His eyes broke away from the orb. It was surrounded by darkness. The dark was also accompanied by cold, - a type of cold that was more intense than what he had felt occasionally from the walls of his demolished room. He turned to go back. Maybe he could fix it somehow; feel warm and safe again; be happy and forget this tragedy that caused him to escape.

Turning around he saw her, the female wolf with the silver grey fur. Her insides spilled across the ground for all to see. Her eyes held open in a horrid stare that could freeze anyone to the bone. His room had been her womb. With his torrid escape to get to his foe, D.C. had ripped her apart. He not only lost his Utopia, but purposefully sacrificed his mother for his own endless rage. For this crime he would surely go to Hell.

- - - -

Howls of the hunting party echoed out of the darkness. D.C. opened his eyes only to have a large black paw scrape its sharp claws across his cheek. The ghost wolf was growling and ready for battle. His swipe was to break D.C. out of his revelations.

Instinctively, D.C. growled back and stood from his crouched position. His rage at the unprovoked blow had hit him on two levels: The first being that D.C. had been content to remain docile and this wolf attacked him; the second was that it reinforced the fact that he was not dreaming. Reality was here and it sucked!

With his rage D.C. felt his body come alive, only this time....he didn't black out the way that he had done before on other nights.

He grew in size to almost seven feet in height. All of his body became fur covered and the fur was grey, like that of his mother. His ears elongated and became more sensitive. His arms and legs bulged with muscle and each paw had longer, sharper, harder claws than before. His blood boiled and his bones cracked, the same way they had when he was removing himself from the womb. He let out a great howl. Not in pain but in ecstasy that could only be felt by embracing the freedom of becoming a werewolf.

The strange man had disappeared, but the large ghost wolf had wrapped itself around D.C.'s body like a shadow. Now they were one and the cuts left on his cheek by the great ghost did not bleed. They glowed silver in the dim moon.

From within the cabin there was rustling around. D.C. put his nose to the air. The rancid smell of "Bane" filled the area. D.C. may have been able to distinctly hear only two individuals inside, but now he knew that the whole place was surrounded. He guessed that there were at least another dozen of these creatures outside.

Thinking clearly D.C. came to comprehend that his getting here had been carefully masked and that Loki told the truth about guiding the hunting party to this place. An impending fight was on its way and somehow, he had to get the hunting party on his side, cut down the evil doers of the woods and the cabin as well as save the life of a young boy.

"Shit!" D.C. grumbled aloud. "It's dark

out!"

Chapter 10

Inside the obscure little cabin, the two men playing cards heard the distant howls. The one looked up at the other. William's face instantly told Butcher that he wasn't put off by the sounds.

"Coyotes calling out," William half snarled as he looked back down at his cards. He was stuck with a handful of rubbish.

Butcher shook his head and stood up. "Those aren't howls of coyotes. I know those howls." He immediately dropped his fangs and extended his claws revealing his vampire nature.

"Werewolves?" questioned

William. He had been told they existed. He was also told that they were so few in numbers that most vampires never actually get to see one.

Butcher, now standing next to the window to look outside, nodded.

William put his cards on the table. He tried to push his ability to hear to its limits. For the moment there was silence echoing back from the woods.

"Do you see anything from the sentries out there?" William finally asked.

Butcher just shook his head. He didn't want to voice his thoughts. Either the others hiding outside had already fallen to the wolf pack or they had fled for their own lives. Butcher knew that one on one, in most encounters with the beasts, a vampire typically won. If the bastards came as a pack, well...he maybe should run off now. Problem with that was there was another car pulling up to the little fort.

Looking at the new arrival he could see that it was his boss. Robert Doulson.

Butcher watched as the man came towards the cabin door. "We're getting some backup."

William just looked at Butcher. He was the novice here, and backup had to be good, it made their little clique stronger. He decided to take another look at his cards.

- - - -

Jeremy sat on the floor wide-eyed at the change in the man's appearance. He heard no howls only their bantering. His eyes grew wider when the door to the cabin burst open and another man strolled in.

"What are you starin' out the window for?" the new addition asked Butcher. He was husky in stature and Jeremy bet he could through his weight around. He wasn't really sure what that meant exactly, but he bet the man could do it.

Butcher answered with caution, "We've heard howling out there. I'm pretty sure it's a wolf pack."

"A wolf pack?" was queried the other man. "Not around here!"

Another howl seemed to cue

from the night outside of the cabin before Butcher could purse his lips to answer.

Jeremy could hear the howl this time as well. He wondered if it was possible for there to be werewolves. He then thought about the stranger, D.C.. Jeremy's eyes bounced around the room looking in all directions yet he wasn't really seeing anything. He bet the odd man who was naked on the river was a werewolf after all; he was just too scared to tell him and his mom. Jeremy imagined D.C. coming out and saying he was a werewolf and his mom screaming and running in terror with him tossed like a sack of potatoes over her shoulder.

"Fuck!" cursed the man who was standing in the doorway. He stood there and pulled out his gun from the holster. The weapon had been tucked in around his torso. Opening the clip he took a look at the bullets. "Are these things silver? Silver works...right?"

Butcher turned his gaze away from the window while turning his head from side to side in a negative manner. "Sorry, but the Sovereign around these parts doesn't give us crap to fight off werewolves. We're better off hoping its just a running pack and that we're not its destination."

These words no sooner flowed from his lips when D.C. let out his howl right next to the house.

The one holding the gun stared at the others with a look of horror. He had never seen a werewolf and had no idea what to expect from the beasts. He just remembered being told that they live for their Gods and their Gods demanded vampire blood. If it was possible, Robert Doulson went paler than pale as his hands shook in the attempt to put his gun back together.

William had dropped his cards again and moved toward the back of the cabin. He didn't realize that is where D.C. was standing, in his full Fenril form, waiting for the hunting pack to arrive.

"Might as well toss that thing away," Butcher said as he tilted his head to point towards the gun in Doulson's hand. "It'll slow them down, but it sounds like you had better suit up for a fight." Stern words of advice from Butcher who now not only had his fangs and claws extended, but you could see his muscles harden and ready to shield himself to the oncoming battle.

"But....but...I was only turned last week," William stammered. He looked toward Doulson for some sort of consoling.

The veteran vamp looked at him and said, "It's been nice knowing ya."

Chapter 11

The hunting party had arrived. The pack only had seven members. Their leader was a large Garu who resembled a coyote more than a wolf. As D.C. watched their approach, only two of the pack looked like the wolves that had initially chased him a year ago when he had murdered his mother as he rid himself of her womb.

They walked casually across the clearing that was there, speaking softly back and forth in their funny language.

"This whole place reeks of bane," a female toward the back protested.

Their leader huffed and then tested the air. "The worm is here," he said with a casual tone.

Another tested the air and added, "Most of it has fled except for what is in the building."

They all nodded at each other.

D.C. watched from the shadows. How was he going to present himself. He was smaller than any other within the pack even though his new transformation had made him larger by at least half of his normal body size. He felt Fenris shadow around him like a suit of armor. D.C. sighed. Now, or never, he told himself as he stepped from the shadows behind the cabin and into the ambient lighting of the clear night. The sun had finally set.

As if a spot light had followed D.C.'s steps, the attention of the pack was instantly upon him. So was their rage.

"Death Cub, " one of them sneered as he was first to leap from the ground and come toward D.C..

Fenris lashed out from around D.C.'s body, and threw off the attack. The other were went flying and landed harshly on his back not knowing what it was that hit him.

The others stared as the great, black God of their beliefs stood between them and D.C. His eyes were a blaze with golden fire. The one he had tossed managed to sit up only to be met directly by the golden fire eyes.

"Great Fenris," the leader chorused as he dropped to his knees in submission. The others followed suit.

"By the ordainment of Loki, my

father, brother to Romulus and Remus, equal to Seth and Gaia, this wolf has redeemed his soul for God."

The others, too frightened to argue against one of their deities, quietly bowed their heads. They all knew the bounty for the head of their "Death Cub" was revoked, -not by their king, Romulus, but by one of their Gods. The God they trusted to help them in battles against the vampires and the bane of the worm.

Fenris, having protected his son from the blood hunt, eyes dimmed and body faded away into the dark.

D.C. looked at each member of the pack as they slowly stood. With a quiet respect they waited for the next stage of their battle. D.C. knew he was the one would be the one initiating this mark.

- - - -

Without a single further sound from outside of the cabin, the thundering crash of the end wall where D.C. had first looked into the cabin was of the boards being broken apart with a pulling force. Through the dust D.C.'s eyes scanned the room to see where Jeremy was.

Jeremy had shut his eyes tightly and was breathing heavily past the gag in his mouth. If the howls hadn't scared him, the guns of the others in the cabin with him did. Of course, watching them transform into monsters and talk about werewolves was of no help either. Clouds of dust caused by the savage entry of what Jeremy understood were werewolves were ticking his nose. He sneezed unwillingly. He struggled to not have attention drawn to him. He was unable to run or even try to get away from this nightmare. All he could do was hope to wake up.

The sound of shattering glass, splintering wood and ripping growls ran through the boy's ears. He cried quietly hoping to go unnoticed. Something wet splattered across his face as he heard cracking and tearing sounds that he did not recognize. He could feel the floor boards' shift and move under him as the conflict ensued beyond his eyelids. Something hit him on the leg and that was when he pissed himself. It was grabbing for him now whatever it was. He just knew it was something horrible, something from one of those movies his mother said he was too young to watch. That's how he was able to figure out this wasn't a nightmare, but a special spot in Hell that he had been brought here to witness.

The scuffle grew louder with what Jeremy could only imagine as more arriving on this scene. There were angry growls of dogs or wolves or something. There were screams of men and a foul yet sweet smell rose all around him. With a thundering bellow there was one final howl and then everything was silent. All grew quiet except for his gasps of air from behind the gag in his mouth. Jeremy still didn't want to open his eyes. If they were done with each other he would have to be next. He was the only thing left. Jeremy could not help but cry harder. No longer was he able to quell the terror.

Jeremy suddenly heard the sounds of soft footsteps moving towards him. He tried to stop crying.

Maybe if he stopped his breathing he could play dead. This was impossible. He was too frightened to attempt such a thing. He thought of his mother and wished he could hug her good-bye.

He could hear the thing crouch near him and he swallowed hard. It had a sickening sweet smell all around it. The pugnacity was too much. Jeremy vomited within his own mouth and only some was able to seep out past the gag. He felt its presence reach out towards him. It was going to grab him and sweep him away.

A deep throaty snarl came baying out of nowhere. Jeremy felt the wind as the looming threat was thwarted. He heard a single scream, cracking noise and was splattered with something wet once more. Jeremy washed down the vomit in his mouth.

A low, deep voice spoke softly into Jeremy's ear, "Keep your eyes closed kid. You don't need to see what's going on here."

Jeremy allowed a flood of tears to come to his eyes. He knew the voice and calmed immediately. It was the man he found on the bank of the river earlier that day. He was here! D.C. wasn't a monster, but an angel.

Jeremy relaxed himself. He was being untied and the gag removed. He reached out and hugged his rescuer, keeping his eyes closed at D.C. request. He did not want to go against the request of an angel!

D.C. easily picked up the boy and carried him out of the remnants of the cabin. The wind that coursed through his nostrils was fresh and scented with more water than anything else. Exhaustion was taking over the boy's body. As the smell of bane lifted, it seemed to D.C. that the boy grew limp as he fell into a slumber.

D.C. met with an elderly woman who was finally joining the hunting pack. She was aged, her eyes blind with that age. She was also hunched with a large bend in her back. The cane she carried was made of oak. Her smile was bright and resonated though D.C. as if she was peering into his very soul. D.C. didn't have to speak. She turned as he walked so that she was able to walk with him. The other pack members followed. All were easily forgetting what had just transpired here at a forgotten cabin, within the woods, along the Potomac River.

The boy lay sleeping peacefully in the crooks of D.C.'s arms. Jeremy knew D.C. would take him home.

Chapter 12

As the dawn broke over the horizon, D.C. stood in solitude at the far end of the hay field. He could barely see the house that belonged to Sharon Miller and her young son Jeremy. His body had returned to its normal form of the half wolf, half man that he had grown accustomed to. His heart sank with the thoughts of the last thirty-six hours.

After gingerly carrying Jeremy home, the old woman who had walked along side of D.C. never questioned where they were going. Upon reaching the farm was the first time she had made any outward gesture towards him.

She placed her hand on D.C.'s

arm. He looked at the strange touch, pondering its meaning. Looking around he could see they were in the field, about half way to the house.

D.C. came to a stop. The old woman smiled. How she was able to see to have been with him all this way and then reach out to him, he did not know. Quietly she began a chant. D.C. felt the air cool. A staggering fog rolled in.

Even though, this strange woman appeared to look human her words were that of the wolf tribe. D.C. was smart enough to know that it was her calling in the cloud bank that was covering the field.

As she continued her chant, D.C. saw with some awe the dirt and splatter lift from the boy. The slight cut inside of his left brow healed with a silent shutting of the skin. Jeremy even appeared to drift into a deeper sleep.

"What are you doing?" D.C. questioned through the fog of his mind. It was getting hard for him to remember the events of the hour before.

The old woman smiled. She gently looked over the boy and laid her hand to rest for a moment on his chest. She could feel the lad breathing deeply and without care. She then removed her hand. Moving her blank eyes towards the face of D.C. she finally spoke. This time she used normal human English words.

"My name is Fayda," she informed him. "I am the Seer of the Garu Nations. I am a Shaman of sorts. I walk with all of the Garu. It does not matter if they are of the Gaia

Tribe of the Earth, following the Nature of Remus, with the yellow eyes, or if they are of the Seth Nation, following the Steel of Romulus, with the blue eyes. I listen to all our Gods. Gaia of the Earth, Seth of the Man, God of all Creations whose name is Jehovah."

D.C.'s confusion must have be mounted upon his features. He knew of God. Mildred and Clive had made sure of that. "What of Fenris?" he asked.

Fayda smiled at him again. "Fenris is our Warrior God. He is the son of Loki. Brother to Romulus and Remus, Loki's adopted pups. He is the one who provided us with our language for which all Garu are able to speak and understand. He has also given us our ability to transform into the knights so that we may fend off the *"bane"* of the Devil."

"Fenris protected me," D.C. stated calmly. He omitted the fact the Loki had announced that Fenris was his father.

Fayda smiled. "Then he had good reason to. I grow old and cannot always see as clearly as I once did, but I can see that you are a good man even if you carry the facade of a demon."

D.C. turned his eyes to the boy sleeping in his arms. Jeremy appeared peaceful as his eyelids fluttered with a dream.

"Take him inside to his bed," Fayda instructed. "I have weaved a spell for him and his mother. They will not remember this night, nor will they remember you."

Tears came to D.C.'s eyes. "I wish they would remember me."

Fayda smiled in a way they showed D.C. that she had left a trick or two unsaid. He didn't bother to ask. He just shifted the boy slightly in his arms and continued on to the farmhouse. He was growing weary himself.

- - - -

A few minutes later, D.C. emerged from the house and saw that there was no one else about. He glanced at the note on the table with the stack of money on it. He still couldn't read the cursive writing on the paper, yet somehow he knew it said that her debt to Robert Doulson was paid and the extra was overpayment she had made.

He walked silently across the field until he had reached the slight knoll almost to the edge of the farmland that was plowed and had some shoots of hay started. This is where he stood for the last four hours, barely moving.

Scenes of the murdered wolf came to his mind. The vision was no longer the grotesque way of his execution. Now, she stood, whole and alive within his mind. Her spirit at rest as his soul had been exonerated. D.C. thought that maybe her spirit was looking lovingly at him, the way a mother should look at her child. The moon in his dream gave way as the sun rose in the sky. The new day had started and the rays of light glistened off the grey fur of his mother. She nodded her head and faded away into the night. D.C. knew that her death would no longer be a nightmare again.

Fayda walked up to D.C.'s side, her long grey hair moving across her face, shoulders and back in the wind. Her right hand clutched the shawl around her shoulders and chest closed. Her oak cane was firmly in the grip of her left hand.

"Will they be okay?" D.C. asked her.

"They will. I have weaved a dream of happiness and now that their woes have been vanquished, they will be happy." She answered.

"And they won't remember," D.C. confirmed with sadness and relief.

She looked at him, "You will

remember. You will carry a fondness in your heart and in your mind, sweet wolf. You will always be grateful for everything they have done for you even if they cannot return the gratitude for everything done for them."

D.C. nodded. It was time to go with his hunters, no, his pack, and be part of the Garu and not an outsider. He still felt Fenris in his shadow. This was no longer troublesome to him. He knew the wolf was an ally.

Fayda fumbled a bit as she turned to shuffle her way back to the edge of the woods where the rest of the pack waited patiently. D.C. helped catch her before she would potentially fall. With her blank eyes she smiled and said, "With the coming of this dawn, also came the redemption of D.C. Hayes."

D.C. smiled back and stated, "Death Cub."

Epilogue

Outside the cabin where Jeremy Miller had been held captive:

William waited until it was dark again before coming out from under the floor boards of the cabin. He had hidden there during the battle between the other vampires and the werewolves. He heard their leader, Robert Doulson, who had wanted the boy held for ransom, have his head ripped from his body along with the others. This included his poker partner, a.k.a. Butcher. He didn't want to suffer this fate so he hid. Being a new vampire he had self-preservation in mind. What ill deeds could he accomplish if he had only been undead for a week?

He carefully stepped past the carnage and into the night air. Looking around he remembered the first wolf, tearing off the end wall of the place as if it was just a toy built out of Popsicle sticks. He didn't see much else except his poker partner jump onto the huge body of the wolf and start to fight back. Briefly, William thought Butcher might win until the second wolf raked it's talons through Butcher's lower back and side, spilling his kidney and other guts out his side. Vampires can heal, and quickly at that, but not if half of their body is removed in a single blow.

There were only shredded bits of clothing here and there that even would give a hint of the vampires that had been here the night before. Anything that had been left here had rapidly dehydrated with the rays of the sun shining through the trees. The werewolves would have taken their heads. William had been taught that decapitating a vampire wasn't enough to kill it. You had to get the head a good distance away from the body, otherwise the fortitude of the vampire could be maintained and allow it to reattach a body part or the head in this case to become whole again. The vampire's blood would burn away too, not leaving any traces behind. Thinking of this he was sure that the werewolves would place the heads out in the sun too. All of his group, from the night before, must surely be dead, in the forever kind of way.

William turned his attention to look over his suit. His sire had given it to him and it was Armani after all. He hoped it had survived his scuffle into his underground hideaway.

Looking the suit over, it was

dirty, but luckily there was no blood. He let out a sigh of relief. A quick dry clean at a hotel on his way back north and no one would be the wiser that he had hidden to save his own ass instead of standing there and getting slaughtered.

Then a new thought came to the forefront of William's brain, "Will I ever just stop breathing?" With this he took off in the fastest run he could muster. Things here at the Potomac River, in the State of West Virginia had not gone according to plan. Now...it was him who would have to break the bad news to Neviah. Not only that she lost a secret financial holding, but it appeared they were hunted out by werewolves!

William gulped air that he didn't need as his thoughts focused more on his sire. He would also have to deal with her rage. He kind of smiled with the thought as he headed northwest towards Michigan. At least after she was done chewing him out for the carelessness of the operation and took stake of the reality of what had happened, she would want to get laid and he liked that. She was better when she was pissed off.

A Few Words from the Author:

D.C. Hayes is a werewolf of a mixed up past and present. I wrote this tale for my husband. I also wrote it for myself.

I have created a whole universe, known as **Darkness Rising**, to express how I feel the creations, workings and powers of the mythical universe work.

I plan on continuing to write and created more stories from this universe, having them entangle themselves into one larger story.

I hope my readers enjoy the ride.

Sincerely:

Alexis Allinson